The Tale of Betsy Butterfly

By
Arthur Scott Bailey

THE TALE OF BETSY BUTTERFLY

I

BEAUTY AND THE BLOSSOMS

EVERY one of the field people in Pleasant Valley, and the forest folk as well, was different from his neighbors. For instance, there was Jasper Jay. He was the noisiest chap for miles around. And there was Peter Mink. Without doubt he was the rudest and most rascally fellow in the whole district. Then there was Freddie Firefly, who was the brightest youngster on the farm — at least after dark, when his light flashed across the meadow.

So it went. One person was wiser than any of his neighbors; another was stupider; and somebody else was always hungrier. But there was one who was the loveliest. Not only was she beautiful to look upon. She was graceful in flight as well. When one saw her flittering among the flowers it was hard to say which was the daintier — the blossoms or Betsy Butterfly.

For that was her name. Whoever gave it to her might have chosen a prettier one. Betsy herself always said that she would have preferred Violet. In the first place, it was the name of a flower. And in the second, her red-and-brown mottled wings had violet tips.

However, a person as charming as Betsy Butterfly did not need worry about her name. Had she been named after a dozen flowers she could have been no more attractive.

People often said that everybody was happier and better just for having Betsy Butterfly in the neighborhood. And some claimed that even the weather couldn't help being fine when Betsy went abroad.

"Why, the sun just has to smile on her!" they would exclaim.

But they were really wrong about that. The truth of the matter was that Betsy Butterfly couldn't abide bad weather — not even a cloudy sky. She said she didn't enjoy flying except in the sunshine. So no one ever saw her except on pleasant days.

To be sure, a few of the field people turned up their noses at Betsy. They were the jealous ones. And they generally pretended that they did not consider Betsy beautiful at all.

"She has too much color," Mehitable Moth remarked one day to Mrs. Ladybug. "Between you and me, I've an idea that it isn't natural. I think she paints her wings!"

"I don't doubt it," said Mrs. Ladybug. "I should think she'd be ashamed of herself." And little Mrs. Ladybug pursed up her lips and looked very severe. And then she declared that she didn't see how people could say Betsy was even good-looking, if they had ever noticed her tongue. "Honestly, her tongue's as long as she is!" Mrs. Ladybug gossiped. "But she knows enough to carry it curled up like a watch-spring, so it isn't generally seen.... You just gaze at her closely, some day when she's sipping nectar from a flower, and you'll see that I know what I'm talking about."

Now, some of those spiteful remarks may have reached Betsy Butterfly's ears. But she never paid the slightest attention to them. When she met Mehitable Moth or Mrs. Ladybug she always said, "How do you do?" and "Isn't this a lovely day?" in the sweetest tone you could imagine.

And of course there was nothing a body could do except to agree with Betsy Butterfly. For it was bound to be a beautiful, bright day, or she wouldn't have been out.

So even those that didn't like Betsy had to give up trying to quarrel with her.

II
JOHNNIE GREEN'S NET

JOHNNIE GREEN was never quite happy unless he was collecting something. One year he went about with a hammer, chipping a piece off almost every rock in Pleasant Valley. And of course he gathered birds' eggs.

After he tired of that he began collecting postage stamps. Next he turned his attention to tobacco tags, even hailing travellers who passed the house, to ask them whether they hadn't a "hard one," meaning by that a tag that was hard to get.

When he felt quite sure that he had a sample of every kind of tobacco tag in the whole world, Johnnie Green had to think of something else to collect. And since it was summer, and a good time to find them, he decided to start a collection of butterflies.

News spreads fast among the field people; and almost as soon as Johnnie Green had made up his mind about his new collection, the whole Butterfly family knew of it.

Old Mr. Crow was the one that first learned of Johnnie's plan. And he was not pleased, either.

"Butterflies!" he scoffed. "I should think Johnnie Green might better spend his time doing something worth while. Butterflies, indeed! Now, if he would only collect Crows there'd be some sense in that!"

But that was before old Mr. Crow and his neighbors understood exactly what a collection was. And the Butterflies felt quite proud because Johnnie Green was going to busy himself with them.

Later, when the field people discovered that collecting Butterflies meant catching them and sticking pins through their heads, the Butterfly family became greatly excited and worried. And as for old Mr. Crow, he was very glad that Johnnie had not decided to collect him and his relations.

Well, if you had been in Pleasant Valley that summer, on almost any fine day you might have seen Johnnie Green running about the fields or the flower garden with a butterfly net in his hand.

He had made the net from a barrel hoop and a piece of mosquito netting, to which he nailed an old broomstick for a handle. And for the first few days when he started making his new collection he didn't visit the swimming hole once. When his father asked him to do a little work for him—such as feeding the chickens, or leading the old horse Ebenezer to water—Johnnie Green was not so pleasant as he might have been. He complained that he was too busy to bother with the farm chores just then.

But Farmer Green told him to run along and do his work.

"You'll have plenty of time to play," said Johnnie's father.

The Butterfly family was sorry that Farmer Green didn't keep his boy at work from dawn till dark. They didn't like to have to watch out for fear that horrid net might swoop down upon them and catch them. They wanted to have a good time among the flowers without being in constant terror of capture at the hands of Johnnie Green.

But, strange to say, Betsy Butterfly was not in the least uneasy. She was so gentle herself that she couldn't believe anybody would harm her.

Little did Betsy realize that she was really in great danger. Her fatal beauty was sure to catch Johnnie Green's eye. And though Betsy Butterfly did not know it, only an accident could prevent her being added to Johnnie Green's collection.

III
A MISHAP

EXCEPT for the work that his father made him do now and then, there was only one thing that bothered Johnnie Green in making his collection of butterflies. The weather was not so good as it might have been. He soon found that there was no use hunting for butterflies except in the sunshine. So when a three days' rain came, Johnnie began to wish he had started a different sort of collection.

But the weather cleared at last. And the sun came out so bright that Johnnie fairly pulled old Ebenezer away from the watering-trough and hustled him back to his stall; for he was in a hurry to get to the flower garden with his butterfly net. As for the chickens, they had very little food that day.

Once in the garden, Johnnie Green found more butterflies than he had ever noticed before. But as soon as he began chasing them, they flew away to the meadow. That is, all but Betsy Butterfly. She said she was sure Johnnie Green wouldn't annoy her.

And that was where she was wrong. The moment he caught sight of her, with her mottled red-and-brown wings with the violet tips, Johnnie cried: "There's a beauty!"

But Betsy Butterfly was so used to such remarks that she paid little heed to him. Even when he crept nearer and nearer to her, with old dog Spot at his heels, she did not take fright.

With her tongue deep in a fragrant blossom she was enjoying its delicious sweetness when Johnnie Green, bearing his net aloft, sprang at her.

When Johnnie jumped, Betsy Butterfly started up in alarm. She had really waited until it was too late. And if something unexpected hadn't happened to Johnnie Green, Betsy would surely have had a place in his collection.

But luckily for her, Johnnie met with a fall. He may have tripped on a vine. Or his foot may have slipped on the wet ground. Anyhow, he fell sprawling among the flowers, dropping his precious net as he stretched out his hands to save himself.

Johnnie's fall gave Betsy Butterfly her only chance. Coiling her long tongue out of her way, she quickly made her escape.

So Johnnie Green lost her. But she was not all that he lost. A strange accident happened just as he fell, for old dog Spot leaped forward at the same time. And, much to his surprise, Spot found his head inside the butterfly net. The long broomstick handle thumped him sharply on his back. And the silly fellow took fright at once.

With yelps of terror he scurried out of the flower garden. And Johnnie picked himself up just in time to see Spot tearing across the meadow toward the woods.

"Spot! Spot! Come back!" Johnnie Green shouted. But old Spot paid no attention to his young master. Perhaps he was too scared to hear him.

Spot wanted to get rid of that net that covered his head. And he knew of no better place to go than the woods where he hoped to be able to free himself from his odd muzzle by rubbing against a tree or nosing among some bushes.

Johnnie ran a little way after him. But when he saw Spot duck into the woods he turned back sadly towards the house. For all he knew, old Spot might run a mile further before he stopped.

Johnnie would have to make a new net if he wanted to catch any more butterflies for his collection.

And the trouble was, he had no more mosquito netting.

A good many of the field people saw old Spot as he dashed off with the butterfly net over his head. And they enjoyed a hearty laugh at the strange sight.

As for Betsy Butterfly, she had learned to watch out for Johnnie Green. And she knew that another time he would have to be twice as spry as he had shown himself, if he expected to capture her.

Old Spot didn't come home till afternoon. When he appeared at last he looked very sheepish. He hoped no one had noticed his fright. And he wouldn't go near the flower garden again for a whole week.

IV
BUSYBODIES

LITTLE Mrs. Ladybug said that she wished Betsy Butterfly no ill luck. But she thought that perhaps it would have been a good thing for her if Johnnie Green had caught her and put her in his collection.

On hearing that strange remark Mehitable Moth turned quite pale. She never wanted Johnnie Green's name mentioned by anyone, because she lived in constant terror for fear he might mistake her for one of the Butterfly family and capture her.

"What do you mean?" she asked Mrs. Ladybug, while fat Jennie Junebug waddled nearer them, in order to hear everything they said. Though Jennie was sleepy, having stayed out very late the night before, the promise of a bit of gossip made her brighten up at once.

"I mean—" said Mrs. Ladybug—"I mean that Johnnie Green would certainly have brushed Betsy Butterfly before adding her to his collection." And then, seeing a blank look on the faces of her hearers, she cried. "Don't tell me you haven't noticed how untidy Betsy Butterfly is! Can it be possible that the airs she gives herself, and her fine manners, have deceived you?"

"What is it?" asked Mehitable Moth breathlessly. And as for Jennie Junebug, her breath was coming so fast that she couldn't say a word.

"I'll tell you exactly what I mean," Mrs. Ladybug continued. "I stopped and spoke to Betsy Butterfly this very morning. And I stepped up close to her, because I wanted to see if she really does paint her wings, as my friend Miss Moth, here, suspects," Mrs. Ladybug explained to Jennie Junebug. "And what do you think? I saw that Betsy Butterfly was completely covered with dust, from head to foot!"

Mehitable Moth looked rather uncomfortable. She was somewhat dusty herself. And she thought that Mrs. Ladybug might be giving her a sly dig.

"Perhaps Betsy had been on a journey," she ventured.

"Ah! But there is no dust to-day, on account of the rain we had last night," Mrs. Ladybug replied. "I'm convinced that the dust I saw on Betsy Butterfly was weeks old."

"The idea!" Jennie Junebug exclaimed. "I should think she'd be ashamed of herself. Did you tell her how untidy she looked?"

Mrs. Ladybug shook her head.

"No!" she answered. "But I've been thinking the matter over. And I believe it's my duty to speak to her about it. I don't see what she's thinking of, to go about looking like that!"

Miss Moth looked more uneasy than ever, especially when Mrs. Ladybug said:

"Wouldn't you like to come with me while I look for Betsy?"

"I must go home now, thank you!" said Mehitable. And she hurried away without another word.

But Jennie Junebug spoke up at once and said she would be delighted to accompany Mrs. Ladybug.

"Really," Jennie confided to her companion, "it's a good thing to have backs as hard and slippery as yours and mine. For the dust can't stick to us as it does to some."

"There's no excuse for not keeping oneself neat," Mrs. Ladybug said severely. "And I shall give Betsy Butterfly a piece of my mind."

V
NO JOKER

MUCH to Mrs. Ladybug's surprise, she did not find Betsy Butterfly in the flower garden.

"It's too bad she's not here," Mrs. Ladybug remarked to her friend Jennie Junebug, who accompanied her. "We'll have to look in the meadow. And it may take a long time to find Betsy there."

Jennie Junebug yawned right in Mrs. Ladybug's face.

"Then I can't come with you," she said. "I'm getting terribly sleepy again. And since I expect to be up all night, I'm going to take a nap."

Mrs. Ladybug looked at Jennie with great disapproval as that fat young person crept under a leaf and went to sleep.

"Things have come to a pretty pass when ladies stay out all night!" she muttered. "It was not that way when I was a girl. But times have changed for the worse."

The longer Mrs. Ladybug stared at her sleeping friend, the more she thought that she ought to wake her up. "If I rouse her she'll be so drowsy to-night that she'll simply have to go to bed," Mrs. Ladybug thought.

So she poked Jennie Junebug several times.

But Jennie Junebug only stirred slightly and murmured something in her sleep.

And seeing that it was useless to try to awaken her Mrs. Ladybug set out for the meadow alone.

The sun hung low in the west when Mrs. Ladybug found Betsy Butterfly among a clump of milk-weed blossoms. But Mrs. Ladybug did not care what time it was. She was satisfied when she saw that Betsy was just as dusty as ever. For, to tell the truth, little Mrs. Ladybug was so jealous of the beautiful Betsy that she wanted to say something disagreeable to her.

"Hasn't this been a lovely day?" Betsy Butterfly cried happily, as soon as she noticed Mrs. Ladybug. "I've enjoyed every moment of it. Ever since I saw you in the flower garden this morning I've been here in the meadow, flitting from one blossom to another."

"You might better have spent a little of your time in a different way," Mrs. Ladybug remarked with a frown.

Betsy Butterfly looked up in surprise, withdrawing her long tongue from the blossom in which she had just buried it.

"Ugh!" A shudder shook prim Mrs. Ladybug. "Please coil your tongue!" she begged. "I can't bear the sight of it. But I must say that I ought not to expect good manners in a person who goes about looking as untidy as you do."

Betsy Butterfly laughed gaily.

"I didn't know you were such a joker!" she exclaimed.

"Oh, I'm not joking," Mrs. Ladybug said. "I mean every word I say."

"Then I wouldn't talk so much, if I were you," Betsy Butterfly advised her with a merry twinkle in her eye. And before Mrs. Ladybug could say another word Betsy Butterfly flew away and left her spluttering and choking.

"She insulted me!" Mrs. Ladybug screamed, as soon as she was able to speak. "She insulted me. And then she hurried off because she didn't dare stay!"

But Mrs. Ladybug was mistaken about one thing. Betsy Butterfly knew that she had just time to reach home before sunset. So that was why she left so suddenly. For she never was willing to travel when the sun was not shining.

"I'll see Betsy in the morning," Mrs. Ladybug promised herself savagely. "I'll make it my business to follow her everywhere she goes, until I've given her a good talking to."

VI
MRS. LADYBUG'S ADVICE

LITTLE did Betsy Butterfly guess what Mrs. Ladybug intended to say to her. And if she had known what it was she would have been merely amused. For Betsy was entirely too sweet-tempered to take offense at anybody's fault-finding—least of all that of Mrs. Ladybug, who was really a good-hearted soul, when she wasn't jealous. And when Betsy went to the flower garden early the next morning she felt kindly towards the whole world, not even excepting Johnnie Green, though he had tried to capture her.

Well, Mrs. Ladybug was waiting for Betsy Butterfly among the flowers. She had been in such haste to reach the garden early that she had not stopped to have her breakfast. And like many people who have not drunk their morning cup of coffee, she was in a very peevish mood.

"Now, Miss Pert, I want you to listen to me!" That was Mrs. Ladybug's greeting to Betsy Butterfly on one of the most delightful days of the whole summer. "It's my unpleasant duty—" said Mrs. Ladybug, who by that time was enjoying herself thoroughly—"it's my unpleasant duty to tell you that people are talking about you. They say that you're going about covered with dust! And as a friend, I advise you to give yourself a thorough brushing each morning, and as often thereafter as may be necessary."

Betsy Butterfly had listened in amazement to Mrs. Ladybug's words. And she had hard work not to laugh, too, because she thought Mrs. Ladybug's advice decidedly funny.

"Thank you very much!" Betsy said most politely. "I'll remember what you've told me."

Somehow Mrs. Ladybug thought that Betsy meant she would follow her advice. And she looked quite pleased.

"I shall expect a great improvement in your appearance the next time I see you," she announced. And with the manner of a person who has just done somebody a good turn she hurried away to get the breakfast that was waiting for her, somewhere.

Then Betsy Butterfly enjoyed a good laugh.

"How ridiculous!" she said to herself. "But I won't tell Mrs. Ladybug of her mistake, because she might feel upset if I did." And you can see, just by that, how kind-hearted Betsy was. She did not even tell her own family about the joke, for fear of hurting Mrs. Ladybug's feelings.

But jealous little Mrs. Ladybug had no such misgivings. She went out of her way to explain to people that if they noticed a change in Betsy Butterfly's appearance, they might thank her for it.... "I told Betsy that she ought to brush the dust off herself," she informed her friends.

Naturally she was displeased when she met Betsy that very afternoon and saw that the dust still lay thick on her wings.

"I believe you actually want to be untidy!" Mrs. Ladybug cried. "And if you aren't going to brush that dust off, I shall do it myself!" And grasping a small Indian paint-brush, the weight of which she could scarcely stagger under, Mrs. Ladybug advanced upon Betsy Butterfly with a determined look in her eye.

"Oh, don't do that!" cried Betsy.

"It's my painful duty to give you a thorough dusting," Mrs. Ladybug declared.

VII

BUTTERFLY BILL

NOW, a crowd had gathered quickly around Betsy Butterfly and Mrs. Ladybug; for the field people are quick to notice anything unusual. And a sprightly young cousin of Betsy's known as Butterfly Bill said to Mrs. Ladybug, with a wink at everybody else:

"I suppose you'll dust the rest of us, too?"

"Only those that need it!" replied Mrs. Ladybug.

"Then you'll have your hands full," Butterfly Bill told her. "Maybe you haven't noticed that every member of the Butterfly family in Pleasant Valley is covered with dust just as Betsy is."

Mrs. Ladybug looked surprised.

"Is that so?" she said faintly.

"It certainly is!" Bill cried. "Maybe you never knew that the dust is what gives us our—ahem—our beautiful colors," he added proudly. "And I warn you that if you so much as touch my lovely cousin with that brush you'll have every one of us fellows in your hair."

Of course poor Mrs. Ladybug was quite bald. But she knew what Butterfly Bill meant. And she was so upset that she promptly let the paint-brush fall to the ground.

Then Betsy's cousin nodded approvingly.

"Now you'd better hurry home," he told Mrs. Ladybug. "There's a rumor around the meadow that your house is on fire. And they say your children are in great danger."

Little Mrs. Ladybug at once fell to weeping.

"It's that horrid Freddie Firefly!" she shrieked. "I've told him to keep away from my home. I've told him that he would set it to blazing with that light of his. But he's forever sneaking around my house as soon as my back is turned."

"There, there! Don't be frightened!" Betsy Butterfly said to her soothingly. "It's only a rumor, you know."

"That's so," Mrs. Ladybug admitted, drying her eyes. "I hear it almost every day, too. But I never can get used to it.... I suppose this is only a false alarm, after all."

"I wouldn't be so sure about that," Butterfly Bill said wickedly, with a shake of his head. "And if I were you I'd look after my own family a little more carefully, instead of troubling myself with other people's affairs."

Several of Bill's friends applauded his speech. But Betsy Butterfly whispered to him to hush.

"Don't you see that Mrs. Ladybug is not quite herself?" she asked him.

But Butterfly Bill was not a person to be easily silenced like that.

"She's a meddling busybody!" he declared. "And it's my opinion that she ought to be put where she'll have to mind her own business."

"Who—me?" called a wheezing voice right in his ear.

Turning, Butterfly Bill saw that it was Jennie Junebug who had spoken to him. She had noticed the crowd from a distance. And she had just arrived, quite out of breath.

Before Betsy Butterfly's cousin Bill could answer, Jennie Junebug actually threatened him.

"If you were talking about me I shall have to knock you down," she declared.

He had heard that Jennie delighted in flying bang into anybody. But he did not know that she indulged in that unladylike trick only after dark.

"Of course I didn't mean you!" he said hastily.

"And I hope you didn't mean my friend Mrs. Ladybug, either," Jennie Junebug added. "For if you did — —"

But Butterfly Bill waited to hear no more. Thoroughly frightened, he sought safety in flight. And as he flew away Mrs. Ladybug couldn't help noticing the dust on his wings.

"They're certainly a peculiar lot — that Butterfly family!" she muttered.

VIII

DO YOU LIKE BUTTER?

AFTER Mrs. Ladybug failed in her attempt to brush the dust off Betsy Butterfly she grew more jealous of Betsy than ever.

It was really a shame that Mrs. Ladybug should feel like that. Usually she was quite harmless, even if she was a busybody and a gossip. But she simply couldn't forgive Betsy Butterfly for being so beautiful. And now Mrs. Ladybug began to neglect her children more than ever, in order to spy upon Betsy in the hope of discovering some new fault in her.

Betsy Butterfly soon noticed that wherever she went she was sure to see Mrs. Ladybug, who had a way of bobbing up in a most startling fashion. But Betsy was always quite polite to the jealous little creature. And she never failed to inquire for her health and that of her children as well, even if she met Mrs. Ladybug a dozen times a day.

For some reason Mrs. Ladybug seemed quite touchy, where her family was concerned.

"You don't need to ask about my children," she told Betsy at last in a somewhat sharp tone. "They are in the best of health. And I'll let you know in case they fall ill.... It's strange," she continued, "how everybody in this neighborhood is always prying into my household affairs."

Betsy Butterfly smiled to herself. She did not care to quarrel with Mrs. Ladybug — nor with anyone else, for that matter. So she abruptly changed the subject.

"Do you like butter?" she asked.

"Why, no!" said Mrs. Ladybug. "I don't care anything about it. At least, I never ate any."

"Then I don't see how you know whether you like it or not," Betsy observed, "unless you've looked into a buttercup to find out."

Mrs. Ladybug was interested, in spite of herself.

"Can a person tell by doing that?" she wanted to know.

"It's a sure way," said Betsy Butterfly. "I was just looking into this buttercup that I'm sitting on when you flew up and spoke to me."

"Do you like butter?" Mrs. Ladybug inquired.

"I'm afraid not," Betsy told her.

"I'd like to try, myself," Mrs. Ladybug exclaimed eagerly. "But I don't know how."

"It's simple enough," Betsy Butterfly replied. "You just look into a buttercup blossom.

"And if it makes your face yellow, then you're fond of butter—whether you ever had any or not."

So Mrs. Ladybug perched herself on a big blossom and peered earnestly into its cup.

"Is my face yellow?" she asked Betsy.

"I do believe it is!" Betsy Butterfly cried.

And Mrs. Ladybug looked much pleased.

"I've always known I had refined tastes," she remarked with a lofty air. "And now I'd like to sample a bit of butter; but I don't know where to find any."

"Butter? They make it at the farmhouse," Betsy informed her.

"Then perhaps Farmer Green's wife will let me have a little," Mrs. Ladybug said hopefully. "I'll go over to the farmhouse at once.... It's too bad you don't like butter, too," she added.

But secretly she was delighted that Betsy Butterfly had looked into a buttercup in vain.

IX

UNEXPECTED NEWS

LITTLE Mrs. Ladybug had a disappointment when she reached the farmhouse. She found, to her dismay, that she couldn't get inside it; for wire screens blocked her way through both doors and windows. And nobody paid the slightest attention to her when she stopped at the buttery window and asked if she couldn't please have a bit of butter.

There was plenty of golden butter right there in plain sight, since it happened to be churning day. And Farmer Green's wife, with her sleeves rolled above her elbows, was working busily on the other side of the window screen.

"I should think she might easily spare me a small sample!" Mrs. Ladybug cried at last. "I'm afraid Farmer Green's wife is stingy."

Mrs. Ladybug hoped that Johnnie Green's mother would hear her remark. But she didn't. And in the end Mrs. Ladybug had to fly away with her longing for butter still unsatisfied.

Meanwhile Betsy Butterfly had been amusing herself in the meadow to her heart's content. To tell the truth, it was rather a relief to be rid of Mrs. Ladybug's society for so long a time. And Betsy hoped that Mrs. Ladybug's errand to the farmhouse would keep that busybody engaged for the rest of the day.

Now, after she left the farmhouse Mrs. Ladybug set out to find Betsy Butterfly again. But meeting Daddy Longlegs near the stone wall, she stopped to gossip with him, telling him how she had learned that she liked butter, and explaining that she had not yet tasted any.

"So you looked into a buttercup to find out, eh?" said Daddy Longlegs. "I'll have to do that, myself. Maybe I've always liked butter, too, without knowing that I do."

"You can't tell till you try," Mrs. Ladybug remarked. "But you mustn't be too sure. You may be disappointed. There's Betsy Butterfly! She doesn't care for butter at all."

"Are you sure about that?" Daddy Longlegs inquired. "Really, I think you must be mistaken, for I saw her with her face just buried in butter this very day."

At first Mrs. Ladybug looked at him in amazement. And then she grew very angry.

"Betsy Butterfly deceived me!" she cried in a shrill voice. "She was afraid that if I knew she ate butter she would have to share it with me.... I'd like to know where she gets her butter," Mrs. Ladybug mused.

"She was standing on some of Farmer Green's, when I saw her," Daddy Longlegs explained.

"Did she ask him for it?" Mrs. Ladybug demanded.

"I don't believe she did," he admitted. "I think she just took it."

A wicked gleam came into Mrs. Ladybug's eyes when she learned that. And she threw up her hands, exclaiming, "She steals! Betsy Butterfly steals butter! When the field people hear the news they won't think she's so fine." And then Mrs. Ladybug turned to Daddy Longlegs once more and demanded whether he knew of anything else that Betsy Butterfly was in the habit of taking from Farmer Green.

"Eggs!" he replied promptly.

"Eggs!" Mrs. Ladybug repeated after him. "Betsy Butterfly steals butter and eggs!"

And before Daddy Longlegs could stop her she had hurried away to spread the news far and wide.

X
THE NIGHT WATCH

LITTLE Mrs. Ladybug stopped everybody she met in the meadow and related how Betsy Butterfly was taking Farmer Green's butter—and his eggs, too—without asking his permission.

"She's going to get some of us into trouble," Mrs. Ladybug informed her neighbors. "Just as likely as not Farmer Green and his wife will think others are stealing from them. Why, I went to the farmhouse to-day and asked for a bit of butter. And what do you think? Mrs. Green pretended not to hear me! I thought it was queer, at the time. But now I know that she's angry with me. She must have missed some of her butter; and she thinks I'm the guilty party." Mrs. Ladybug shook her finger at her neighbors. "We'll have to do something to put a stop to Betsy Butterfly's thieving," she declared.

Jealous Mrs. Ladybug's story amazed all the field people. They could scarcely believe that anyone so beautiful and dainty as Betsy Butterfly would bemean herself by robbing Farmer Green—or anybody else. But Mrs. Ladybug said that Daddy Longlegs had seen Betsy with her face buried in Farmer Green's butter. And no one could doubt the word of so respectable a person as Daddy Longlegs.

"What steps do you think we ought to take to prevent Betsy from eating any more butter and eggs that don't belong to her?" asked the queen of the Bumblebee family.

"I think we ought to set a careful watch on her," said Mrs. Ladybug. "I'm sure I don't see when she gets her stolen goods, because I've watched her very closely myself for some time. And I've seen her dine on nothing but flowers."

"Perhaps she goes to the farmhouse at night," Jennie Junebug suggested.

"That's a happy thought!" said Mrs. Ladybug approvingly. "We'll have to get Freddie Firefly to follow her about after dark."

So Mrs. Ladybug and her neighbors made arrangements with Freddie Firefly to have Betsy Butterfly spied upon that very night.

"I'll watch her till sunset," Mrs. Ladybug agreed. "And then you must relieve me," she told Freddie. "Don't let her out of your sight until sunrise!" she warned him.

Freddie Firefly promised that he would be faithful to his trust. And later that afternoon, when the sun began to drop behind the mountains, he relieved Mrs. Ladybug, who had been spying upon Betsy ever since their talk earlier in the day.

"She's behaved herself fairly well so far," Mrs. Ladybug whispered to Freddie, as she prepared to fly home to her children. "But there's no knowing when she may start for the farmhouse. So you mustn't take your eyes off her all night long!"

"You can trust me," Freddie assured her. And then Mrs. Ladybug said good evening.

Freddie Firefly always claimed that that was the longest night he ever spent. And he said that if he had realized that he would have to stay in one place from sunset to dawn he never would have agreed to watch Betsy Butterfly.

For Betsy Butterfly went to sleep the moment the sun went down. Freddie had to remain for hours and hours where he could flash his light upon her. And all the while he knew that his whole family was having a delightful time dancing in the hollow over towards the swamp.

It was especially hard for Freddie because he could see the gay lights of the Fireflies twinkling through the dark.

But Betsy Butterfly knew nothing of his long vigil. She slept and slept the whole night long. And Freddie Firefly had to admit to himself, as he watched her, that she didn't act like a robber in the least.

XI

A SLY ONE

WHEN Freddie Firefly reported to Mrs. Ladybug and her neighbors that Betsy Butterfly had taken neither butter nor eggs from Farmer Green during the night the field people were much puzzled.

"She's certainly a sly one!" Mrs. Ladybug exclaimed. "What do you think we ought to do now?" she asked Daddy Longlegs, who was supposed to be very old, and therefore very wise.

"I think you ought to warn her," he replied, after some thought. "You ought to tell Betsy Butterfly that she must stop pilfering."

"No doubt your advice is good," Mrs. Ladybug observed. "And I'll speak to Betsy this very morning.... You must come with me," she told Daddy. "I naturally want to have a witness."

"Oh, I'll come!" he cried in his thin, quavering voice, though what she meant by a "witness" was more than he knew.

So Mrs. Ladybug and Daddy Longlegs set forth to find Betsy Butterfly. And behind them followed a crowd of their neighbors. Even lazy Buster Bumblebee joined the procession. Though he was a drone, and never worked, he was always ready to exert himself for the sake of any new excitement.

The strange company wandered back and forth across the meadow for some time without finding Betsy Butterfly. But at last Mrs. Ladybug spied her. And soon Betsy found herself surrounded by the mob.

"Goodness!" she cried, looking about her in surprise. "How nice of you all to call on me! I'mso glad to see you!"

Betsy Butterfly was so cordial that Mrs. Ladybug couldn't help looking somewhat uncomfortable. She couldn't avoid a strange feeling of guilt. And yet she told herself that Betsy Butterfly was really the guilty one.

"She's a bold piece!" Mrs. Ladybug exclaimed, under her breath.

"Perhaps you won't be so happy to see us when you hear what we have to say to you," Mrs. Ladybug began.

"There hasn't been an accident, I hope!" Betsy cried. "Your house hasn't burned?"

"No!" replied Mrs. Ladybug. And again she said, "No!" in a very decided manner. "We've come to warn you that we've found out about your trickery," she announced. "We know that you like butter, and that you're in the habit of taking it from Farmer Green—yes! and eggs, too!"

"Why, I don't know what you're talking about!" Betsy Butterfly faltered. She was really greatly surprised.

"It won't help you to be untruthful," Mrs. Ladybug told her severely. "It's no wonder—" she added—"it's no wonder Mrs. Green wouldn't give me a bit of butter when I went to the farmhouse yesterday. She thought I was the one that's been stealing it from her, right along."

And then Mrs. Ladybug was amazed by what followed. For Betsy Butterfly actually smiled at her.

"You're mistaken," she said. "I never eat butter. I don't like it. And as for eggs, how could I ever break through an egg-shell?"

"I don't know anything about that," said Mrs. Ladybug. "And besides, I didn't come here to be questioned," she added tartly. "If you have any questions to ask, just ask 'em of him, for he's seen you with your face buried in butter!" And she pointed at Daddy Longlegs.

And now it was his turn to look uncomfortable. For he considered Betsy Butterfly to be very beautiful indeed.

XII

A TERRIBLE BLUNDER

WHEN the beautiful Betsy Butterfly turned her gaze on him, Daddy Longlegs couldn't help wishing that he had worn his new coat that day. However, he straightened his necktie carefully and tried to look as well as he could.

"So you've seen me eating butter, have you?" Betsy Butterfly asked him.

"Not eating it!" he corrected her. "I've seen you standing on it. And your face was hidden in it, too."

Mrs. Ladybug shot a triumphant glance at the crowd, of which she and Betsy Butterfly and Daddy Longlegs were the center.

"What have you to say now, my fine lady?" she demanded of Betsy with a sneer.

And still Betsy Butterfly was quite unruffled.

"Where did you see me doing that?" she asked Daddy Longlegs pleasantly enough.

"I object!" Mrs. Ladybug interrupted hastily. "You needn't answer her question," she advised Daddy Longlegs. "I know her tricks! She'll keep us talking here until we forget what our errand was!"

But Daddy Longlegs paid no attention to Mrs. Ladybug's advice.

"I saw you in this meadow," he explained.

And Mrs. Ladybug began to look somewhat worried.

"Come!" she cried. "Let's all go home now. We've warned her; and we'll leave her to think over what she's done.... I hope—" Mrs. Ladybug added, turning to Betsy Butterfly—"I hope you'll decide to turn over a new leaf."

"Why, that's exactly what she did, that time when I saw her!" Daddy Longlegs shouted. "While I was watching her I saw her turn over a leaf. So what's the use of her turning over another."

And now it was Mrs. Ladybug's turn to look amazed and bewildered.

"I don't know what you're talking about," she snapped, glaring at Daddy Longlegs. "And I don't believe you know, yourself."

"Oh! yes, I do!" he retorted shrilly.

"Butter has no leaves," said Mrs. Ladybug with a knowing air. "I saw heaps and heaps of it in Farmer Green's buttery yesterday. And there wasn't a leaf on it."

"How about eggs, then?" shouted somebody in the crowd. It was stupid Buster Bumblebee! And of course nobody paid any heed to his silly question.

As he stared at Mrs. Ladybug dully Daddy Longlegs let his mouth fall wide open.

"Why, what do you mean?" he demanded at last. "You and I aren't talking about the same sort of butter at all! You're describing the kind of butter that Mrs. Green makes at the farmhouse."

"And what, pray tell, have you been talking about all this time?" Mrs. Ladybug gasped.

"The butter-and-eggs in the meadow!" Daddy Longlegs informed her. "I suppose you know the plant, don't you?"

"I've heard of it," Mrs. Ladybug replied. "But I doubt if there is such a thing."

"And I say there is!" Buster Bumblebee clamored. "We Bumblebees are very fond of butter-and-eggs. And we're about the only field people that know how to open a blossom and reach its nectar."

Little Mrs. Ladybug waited to hear no more.

"You've made a terrible blunder!" she told Daddy Longlegs hurriedly. And before he could answer her she had hastened away.

Like many another jealous body, Mrs. Ladybug had behaved very foolishly. And it was no wonder that she wanted to get away from the crowd.

She didn't even beg Betsy Butterfly's pardon for calling her a thief. But all the rest of the field people realized at last that Betsy was no thief.

The butter-and-eggs plant, they were well aware, was as free as the clover, or the milk-weed blossoms, or any other of the wild flowers. Everybody knew that Farmer Green laid no claim to them, though they did grow in his meadow.

And when Betsy Butterfly thanked Daddy Longlegs for his explanation he wished more than ever that he had worn his new coat that day—and his new hat, too.

XIII

THE FRIENDLY STRANGER

OF course, anyone so beautiful as Betsy Butterfly was bound to attract attention. Wherever she went people turned their heads—if they could—to look at her. And those whose heads were so fastened to their bodies that they simply couldn't crane their necks at anybody—even those unlucky creatures wheeled themselves about in order to gaze at Betsy.

If they happened to be ladies they stared at her because they wanted to see what was the latest style in gowns, or maybe hats. And if they happened to be gentlemen they looked at her because they just couldn't help it.

It was no wonder, then, that Betsy Butterfly had many admirers. In fact, she was so accustomed to their flittering after her that usually she paid little heed to them. But now and then one of them made himself so agreeable that Betsy favored him slightly more than the others.

Such was a stranger dressed in yellowish brown whom she chanced to meet among the flowers one day. He was flying from flower to flower with a loud buzzing. And he reminded Betsy Butterfly of somebody, but she couldn't just think who it was.

"Ah!" said the stranger, as soon as he caught Betsy's eye. "The blossoms are fine and fresh after last night's shower, aren't they?"

Betsy had to admit that what the stranger said was true. And when he came right over to the flower where she was breakfasting and began buzzing around her, and eating pollen, Betsy Butterfly thought that for a stranger he seemed very friendly.

She looked at him for a time, out of the corner of her eye, while she tried to recall whom the newcomer resembled. But he looked like no one she had even seen. And then all at once Betsy knew what was so familiar about him. It was his voice!

"You remind me of a friend of mine," she remarked. "He lives in the meadow not far from here. It's your buzzing," she explained. "If I didn't see you I should think you were Buster Bumblebee."

Betsy's remark seemed to please the stranger. And he smiled smugly while he buzzed louder than ever.

"It's not surprising that I make you think of him," he observed. "Indeed it would be odd if I didn't, for I'm a sort of cousin of Buster's, so to speak. Perhaps you didn't know that my name is Bumble—Joseph Bumble."

Naturally Betsy and Joseph became good friends on the spot. And after that people often saw them rambling together among the flowers.

Now, Joseph Bumble proved to be a great talker. And since Betsy Butterfly was an excellent listener, they spent many agreeable hours together.

At least, Joseph enjoyed every minute that he spent in Betsy Butterfly's company. And if at times she found his prattle a bit tiresome, she was too well-mannered to say so.

If the truth were known, Joseph Bumble proved to be somewhat of a braggart. He was forever boasting of his connection with the Bumblebee family. And Betsy couldn't say anything to him without his remarking that his cousin Buster Bumblebee's mother, the well-known Queen, thought this or that.

"And being of royal blood, the Queen ought to know what's what," he frequently said.

"I suppose—" Betsy said to him at last—"I suppose you're of royal blood yourself, Mr. Bumble?"

"Oh, very!" he replied with a smirk. "We're all of us very royal indeed."

And Betsy Butterfly thought how pleasant it was to be friends with anyone who came from such a fine family as Joseph Bumble's.

XIV

A DEEP PLOT

AS time passed, Betsy continued to see a great deal of Joseph Bumble. And she noticed one peculiar thing: Although he talked continually of his cousin Buster Bumblebee, the Queen's son, no one had ever seen the two together.

"How does it happen," she asked Joseph at last, "that I never find you with your cousin? Aren't you friends?"

"We're certainly not enemies," said Joseph Bumble, "though I must admit that we're not quite so intimate as we might be. You see, Buster and I have different tastes. And now that the red clover is in blossom he spends all his time in the clover field. But as you know, like you I am very fond of flowers. And I'd far rather be here in the meadow — or the flower garden — with you, than in the clover patch with Buster Bumblebee."

Naturally such an answer was bound to please Betsy Butterfly. And after that she bothered her head no more about the friendship between the two cousins. Certainly Joseph Bumble's explanation sounded reasonable. And she had no cause to doubt his statement.

Meanwhile there were others among Betsy Butterfly's admirers who became very peevish on observing how much time Betsy and the newcomer in the neighborhood, Joseph Bumble, were spending in each other's society. And they agreed among themselves that something ought to be done to put an end to the upstart Bumble's boasting.

"Betsy Butterfly thinks the fellow is a cousin of Buster Bumblebee's," said Chirpy Cricket. "But I've noticed that he and Buster are never together. Let's ask Buster to come over to the meadow so that he may meet this cousin of his! And then perhaps we'll learn something more about Joseph Bumble than we know now."

Everybody said that that was a good plan. And Betsy's admirers chose Daddy Longlegs to call on Buster Bumblebee and invite him to a party to be given in the meadow the following day.

Daddy Longlegs agreed to do the errand, in spite of the fact that for him it was half a day's journey to the Bumblebee's home from the stone wall where he lived. But he thought that by hurrying he ought to be able to get back in time to put on his best coat and go to the party, though he might arrive somewhat late.

"Don't forget to ask Betsy Butterfly to the party!" Daddy called, as he started off on his long trip.

"Don't worry! I'll attend to that myself," Chirpy Cricket promised.

"And don't forget to invite Joseph Bumble!" Daddy cautioned him.

"Oh! we don't need to ask him," said Chirpy Cricket. "He'll come without being invited, unless I'm greatly mistaken."

Luckily for Daddy Longlegs there was not a breath of wind either that day or the following one. So he made excellent time to the Bumblebee home, where he found Buster Bumblebee and gave him his invitation. Then Daddy turned around and started back towards his stone wall. Buster Bumblebee had promised to come to the party. And Daddy wanted to be present when the two cousins, Buster Bumblebee and Joseph Bumble, met—with Betsy Butterfly right there to watch them.

XV
JOSEPH BUMBLE'S COMPLAINT

IT happened just as Chirpy Cricket had expected. Betsy Butterfly arrived at the party with her admirer, Joseph Bumble, buzzing close behind her. Although he had not been invited, he did not feel the least bit shy about coming.

"Being of a royal family, I never wait to be asked to a place," he had explained loftily to Betsy. "And you'll see that everybody will be glad to see me at the party. People always consider it an honor to have me at their entertainments."

Joseph's words proved partly true, anyhow. Anyone could see that Joseph Bumble was more than welcome. Chirpy Cricket and Daddy Longlegs — as well good many others — rushed up to him and told him how pleased they were to see him.

And Joseph Bumble was having a very agreeable time talking in a loud voice about himself and his family when he suddenly stopped short. A look of displeasure crossed his face. And Daddy Longlegs asked him if he had eaten something that disagreed with him.

"No!" replied Joseph Bumble. "I've been interrupted. And it's hardly the sort of treatment a person of royal blood — like myself — expects to receive at a party."

"Who interrupted you?" Chirpy Cricket inquired.

"I don't know," Joseph Bumble answered. "But someone was talking in a loud voice."

"Are you sure it wasn't yourself that you heard?" Daddy Longlegs wanted to know.

"Certainly not!" cried Joseph. "Don't be silly! Don't you suppose I know my own voice when I hear it?"

"Perhaps it was your echo that you heard," Daddy ventured.

At that Joseph Bumble rudely turned his back on him and began whispering to Chirpy Cricket. He was actually suggesting that Daddy Longlegs should be thrown out of the party!

And then Mr. Bumble again paused abruptly and listened.

"There!" he said to Chirpy Cricket. "Don't you hear that buzzing? That's the person that interrupted me. And I'd like to have him put out of the party too, along with this queer old chap who insulted me a moment ago."

Chirpy Cricket looked around, until his eye rested on Buster Bumblebee, who had just arrived and who was at that moment talking with Betsy Butterfly.

"There's the young man you hear!" Chirpy told Joseph Bumble. "Don't you know him?"

"No!" replied Joseph, as his eyes followed Chirpy Cricket's. "And I don't want to know him, either. He looks to me to be a very ordinary person. And anybody can see that he's annoying Betsy Butterfly. I tell you, I want him chased away from here at once. For I'm of royal blood; and I'm not accustomed to go to parties with ragtags and bobtails. I'm a cousin of Buster Bumblebee, the Queen's son."

Well, Chirpy Cricket tried hard not to laugh right in Joseph Bumble's face.

"I'll see what I can do," Chirpy promised him. "And I will admit that somebody ought to be barred out of this party."

"Good!" exclaimed Joseph Bumble. "I'm glad to know that you're so sensible."

Perhaps he would have spoken in a different fashion had he known exactly what Chirpy Cricket had in mind. But now he said nothing more, though he continued to stare angrily at Buster Bumblebee, who was glad to see Betsy Butterfly, and was telling her as much, too.

XVI

NOTHING BUT A FRAUD

AT last Joseph Bumble's displeasure passed all control. He began to buzz as loud as he could, hoping to drown Buster Bumblebee's buzzing, so that Buster could no longer talk to Betsy Butterfly.

Naturally, Buster soon had to raise his own voice, in order to make himself heard. And soon the two made such a roar that everybody else had to stop up his ears.

Noticing a look of distress on Betsy Butterfly's face, Buster asked her what the trouble was.

"You and your cousin Joseph are making a terrible racket," she told him.

"My cousin Joseph!" cried Buster Bumblebee. "And who is he, I should like to know? Point him out to me, please! For I didn't know I had a cousin at this party."

"There he is!" said Betsy Butterfly, nodding her head towards the glowering Joseph.

"What! That unshaven stranger in the yellowish-brown suit?" cried Buster Bumblebee. "I assure you he's no relation of mine."

"You must be mistaken," Betsy persisted. "He says he's your cousin, and of royal blood himself."

"Nonsense!" cried Buster Bumblebee. "Just let me talk to him a moment, and I'll soon prove that your friend is nothing but a fraud."

Accordingly Buster left her, and straightway perched himself upon a daisy directly in front of Joseph Bumble.

"How-dy do!" said Buster. "I hear you've been talking about me."

Now, Joseph Bumble's only thought was that the noisy chap in the yellow and black velvet must have overheard what he had said to Chirpy Cricket about throwing him out of the party.

"I don't care to talk with you," Joseph announced in his grandest manner. "I'm from such a fine family that I have to be very particular about whom I'm seen with."

"Is that so?" said Buster. "I suppose if Buster Bumblebee were at this party you'd be glad to talk with him?"

"I should say I would!" was the other's answer. "He's my cousin."

"What's your name, anyhow?" Buster Inquired.

"Joseph Bumble!"

"What's the rest of it?" Buster Bumblebee demanded, while the whole company surged around him, so that they might hear.

"I refuse to answer!" said Joseph Bumble. And afterward Daddy Longlegs declared that at that moment he saw the fellow's knees trembling.

"Come!" said Joseph Bumble, turning suddenly to Betsy Butterfly. "I see that we've accidentally fallen in with some rough people; and we'd better be moving on."

But Betsy Butterfly didn't even look at Joseph.

"What is his full name?" she asked Buster.

"He's a Bumble Flower-Beetle," Buster said. "And as for his being related to me, that's all humbug. This stranger is no kin either to the Bumblebee or any other Bee family. But his voice is so much like ours that he's taken part of our name, though our family has always claimed that he has no right to it."

"Who are you?" Joseph Bumble demanded of Buster quite fiercely. He was determined to put his enemy to rout if he could.

"I'm Buster Bumblebee!" was the reply. "Don't you know your cousin?"

When he heard that, Joseph Bumble knew at once that the game was up. His trickery was discovered beyond a doubt. So with one last lingering look at the beautiful Betsy he took to his wings. And no one ever saw him in those parts again.

As for Betsy Butterfly, she never could bear, after that, to hear the name of Joseph Bumble so much as mentioned.

XVII
DUSTY'S DIFFICULTY

IT was to be expected that as time went on, Betsy Butterfly's fame would spread far and wide. And long before the summer was over, half the creatures that lived in Pleasant Valley knew her. They were the ones that went about by daylight and rested at night.

As for the other half—the night-prowlers—many of them had heard about the beautiful Betsy, though of course they had never seen her. That is, none of them had set eyes on her except Freddie Firefly, who had flashed his light upon Betsy all one night, because Mrs. Ladybug had a strange notion that she was stealing butter from the farmhouse.

In fact, after that happened, Freddie Firefly had gone about telling all his friends how beautiful Betsy Butterfly was, and saying what a pity it was that she didn't like moonlight as well as sunshine.

He talked so much about her that at last a good many of the night-prowling people said that they wished they might see Betsy Butterfly just once, for they could scarcely believe that anybody could be as dainty and bewitching as Freddie Firefly would have them believe her.

And there was one dashing young chap of the Moth family who became especially eager to make Betsy's acquaintance. Indeed, he began to complain that he was losing his appetite, through thinking about Betsy Butterfly. So he besought Freddie Firefly to help him out of his difficulty.

Now, while he was talking with Freddie Firefly, this young Moth, who was known as Dusty, never once stopped eating. Freddie Firefly noticed how his fat sides stuck out.

And he wondered what the fellow's appetite could have been like before he lost some of it.

"You don't act like one in delicate health," Freddie Firefly observed, as he watched the greedy Dusty consume more food.

"Oh, but I am!" Dusty Moth protested feebly. "I'm so weak now that I can hardly raise myself with my wings."

Freddie was sure that Dusty's trouble was merely due to his being too fat. But he saw no reason for quarreling with him.

"Can't you think of some plan by which I could meet Betsy Butterfly?" Dusty Moth persisted. "Perhaps if I could see her just once I'd be able to get my mind off her—and on my meals again."

"I don't know how I can help you," Freddie Firefly confessed. "You see, Betsy goes home exactly at sunset. And at present she never seems to make her home in the same place for even two nights. So one can never be sure where she will be.

"Of course, when the sun is shining you can always find her among the flowers. But that won't help you any, because you're such a sleepy-head in the daytime that you couldn't see anything even if it was stuck right into your eyes."

"Can't you explain my sad case to Betsy Butterfly?" Dusty Moth asked hopefully. "I've heard that she's very kind-hearted. And if she knew how I'm suffering on her account I'm sure she'd be glad to meet me some pleasant, dark night."

He begged so piteously that in the end Freddie Firefly agreed to do what he could.

"But I warn you—" he said—"I warn you that I can't give you much hope."

XVIII

SOLOMON OWL'S IDEA

FREDDIE FIREFLY actually did send a message to Betsy Butterfly, telling her that Dusty Moth wanted to see her, and saying that unless she would agree to meet him in the meadow some night soon, Dusty was afraid he would lose his appetite entirely.

But Betsy thought the whole affair was only a joke. So she merely laughed—and sent Freddie no answer at all; for she hardly believed that she needed to explain to him that nothing could induce her to stir out after sunset.

Freddie Firefly was much upset because he received no answer to his message. Perhaps he would not have cared so much had Dusty Moth not made his life miserable each night from dusk to dawn. But that persistent fellow kept asking Freddie every few minutes if he had "heard from her" yet. And naturally anyone would grow tired if he had to keep saying "No! no! no!" all night long.

At the same time Dusty Moth kept insisting in a most annoying way that if he lost much more of his appetite he would be ill, and it would be Freddie Firefly's fault.

So Freddie Firefly began to worry. He came finally to detest Dusty Moth. And Freddie's family noticed that he was growing quite thin, because Dusty Moth left him little time—between questions—in which to eat his meals comfortably.

"I declare, I wish Betsy Butterfly would move away from Pleasant Valley!" Freddie Firefly exclaimed at last, quite out of patience with everybody and everything. "I'm in a pretty fix, I am! And since I don't know how to get rid of this annoying Dusty Moth, I'm going to ask Solomon Owl what I'd better do." That, at least, was a comforting thought.

So the following morning, just before dawn, he made what might be termed a flying call on Solomon Owl who lived in the hemlock woods beyond the swamp.

And luckily wise old Solomon thought of a good plan at once. As soon as he had heard Freddie Firefly's story he said to him:

"If Betsy Butterfly refuses to meet your friend, why don't you ask her for her picture?"

"That's a splendid idea!" Freddie cried. "How in the world did you ever happen to think of it, Mr. Owl?"

Solomon Owl hooted at that question.

"That's my secret," he said. "If I told all I know, everybody else would be just as wise as I am." And after giving another long string of hoots, which he followed with a burst of loud laughter, Solomon Owl popped into his house.

Anyhow, Freddie Firefly couldn't complain, for he now had a remedy for his trouble. And he felt so carefree and happy again that on his way across the meadow he stopped to talk with Jimmy Rabbit, who was taking a stroll in the direction of Farmer Green's cabbage patch.

Freddie Firefly quickly told Jimmy all about his affair with Dusty Moth. He even explained how he had gone to ask Solomon Owl's help, and related what that wise bird had advised.

"There's only one thing that worries me now," said Freddie Firefly anxiously. "I'm wondering whether Betsy Butterfly has ever had a picture made of herself."

XIX

A BIT OF LUCK

JIMMY RABBIT promptly set Freddie Firefly's fears at rest.

"I happen to know," said he, "that Betsy Butterfly has a picture of herself."

"Are you sure?" Freddie asked him eagerly.

"I ought to be," replied Jimmy Rabbit, "because I painted it myself, the very next day after I finished a portrait of old Mr. Crow."

"It ought to be a good one, if you made it," said Freddie. "But wasn't it some time ago that you were an artist?"

"It was earlier in the summer," Jimmy Rabbit admitted. "Of course, Betsy Butterfly has changed somewhat since then. But this picture was a fine likeness of her at the time I painted it.... I suppose," he added, "I was the first one in the whole valley to perceive that she was going to be a beauty when she got her full growth."

"Do you suppose she'll send me the picture, if I ask her, so I can show it to Dusty Moth?" Freddie asked.

Jimmy Rabbit looked a bit doubtful. He pondered for a few moments. And then he said:

"I'll tell you what I'll do! To-morrow morning I'll see Betsy and I've no doubt that she'll loan me the picture if I promise to return it to her."

"That'll be great!" cried Freddie. "Meet me near the duck pond as soon as it's dark to-morrow night; and be sure to bring Betsy's picture with you!"

Then Freddie Firefly hurried off to find Dusty Moth, who happened likewise to be looking for him, because he had a question to ask.

They met shortly. And Dusty Moth immediately cried:

"Have you heard from her?"—meaning Betsy Butterfly, of course.

"Now, see here!" Freddie Firefly said. "It's plain enough that Betsy doesn't care to meet you. But I have a plan that ought to suit you well enough. If you could look at her picture once you'd be satisfied, wouldn't you?"

"I would—" replied Dusty Moth—"if I got my appetite back afterward."

"Well, will you promise to stop pestering me about Betsy Butterfly if I let you see this picture of her?"

"Yes! yes!" Dusty promised impatiently. "Where is it? Quick! Let me see it!"

"Oh! You'll have to wait till to-morrow night," Freddie explained.

"I shall not be able to eat a single mouthful till then!" Dusty Moth groaned.

"Well—you can suit yourself about that," Freddie told him impatiently. "And please don't speak to me again to-night! I've been troubled enough on your account without being bothered by you any more."

"One moment!" cried Dusty, as Freddie Firefly started to leave him.

"Well—what do you want now?" Freddie growled, flashing his light impatiently in Dusty Moth's eyes.

"Are you sure she will let you take the picture?" Dusty asked him.

"Yes! yes! Of course she will! Why shouldn't she, I should like to know? You certainly do ask the silliest questions!"

And yet Freddie Firefly had put the same query himself, to Jimmy Rabbit, only a short time before. But now he was quite certain that his worries were almost at an end.

"Betsy Butterfly has caused me a powerful lot of trouble!" Freddie grumbled, as he hurried over the hollow, to join in the dance of the Firefly family.

XX

SOMETHING SEEMS WRONG

WHEN Jimmy Rabbit went to see Betsy Butterfly the next morning he found her quite willing to let him take her picture away with him.

"But I must say—" Betsy remarked—"I must say that I don't understand why anybody should want to borrow this old portrait. Everyone tells me I have changed a great deal since you made it."

"That's true," Jimmy Rabbit agreed. "But the person to whom I'm going to show it won't know the difference."

"I don't believe he knows me, then," she remarked.

"No! And probably he never will," said Jimmy Rabbit. "But don't you worry about that! From what I hear of him, he's a good deal of a bore."

"Don't bother to bring back that picture!" she called to Jimmy Rabbit as he hopped away.

"I'm afraid Betsy Butterfly is growing vain," he murmured to himself. "To be sure, she haschanged. But I shall always like this portrait of her, because I painted it myself."

Later, when he was in Farmer Green's garden, he wrapped the picture carefully in a rhubarb leaf and hid it beneath a pile of brush. And he didn't come back for it until after dark, just as the moon peeped above the rim of the hills.

At the duck pond Jimmy Rabbit found Freddie Firefly waiting for him, hopping up and down and flashing his light through the misty gloom.

"Did you get it?" Freddie demanded.

"It's safe in my pocket," Jimmy assured him.

"Let me have it!" said Freddie. "Dusty Moth is waiting for me at the fence-corner, near the orchard. And I want to give him a good look at Betsy

Butterfly's picture before the moon gets too high, for he can't see well if there's too much light."

Jimmy Rabbit drew the picture carefully from his pocket. And Freddie Firefly took it and slung it across his back. He fairly staggered under the weight.

"Aren't you going to look at Betsy's picture yourself?" Jimmy Rabbit asked him. "It's a good bit of work, if I do say so."

"Oh! I don't care about seeing it. It's nothing to me, you know," said Freddie carelessly. "But I hope Dusty Moth will be satisfied with it."

"Well, I won't go with you, to see if he is," Jimmy Rabbit told him. "I usually have a light lunch at this hour. So I'll meet you here at the duck pond after I come back from the cabbage patch."

They parted then. And shortly afterward Freddie Firefly dropped down beside Dusty Moth, who made no attempt to conceal his pleasure.

"At last!" he cried. "At last I am to behold the beautiful Betsy Butterfly's picture!... I do hope it's a good likeness!" he added as he began, with trembling hands, to unwrap the rhubarb covering from the portrait.

"It certainly is," Freddie Firefly assured him. "It was made by a friend of mine, who once painted a famous picture of old Mr. Crow."

While Freddie danced along the top of the fence, Dusty Moth carried the picture into the shade of an apple tree, out of the moonlight, so that he might see it more clearly.

A few moments later Freddie Firefly was both surprised and alarmed to hear a cry of anguish from the direction of the apple tree.

"What's the matter?" he called. "There's nothing wrong, I hope?"

But Dusty Moth made no reply.

XXI

A STRANGE CHANGE

RECEIVING no answer to his question, Freddie Firefly skipped down from the fence and sought the shade of the apple tree, where he found Dusty Moth staring fixedly at Betsy Butterfly's picture.

Dusty's face wore a most curious look; he seemed at once angry, sorrowful and amazed. And not till Freddie Firefly asked again what was the trouble did Dusty Moth say a word.

Then he pointed scornfully toward the portrait that Jimmy Rabbit had made earlier in the summer.

"So that's the charming Betsy Butterfly, eh?" he roared. "That's the beauty I've heard so much about! I can tell you right now that if I had any idea she looked like this I never would have lost my appetite over her!"

"You astonish me!" Freddie Firefly exclaimed. "Have you forgotten how anxious you were to meet the lady?"

"Meet her!" Dusty Moth howled. "I promise you I'd never go out of my way to meet anybody that looked as she does—though I might go a long distance to avoid her."

Freddie Firefly glanced toward the picture. But it had fallen face downward upon the ground. And he did not take the trouble to raise it.

"Well, you think Betsy Butterfly is beautiful, don't you?" he asked.

"Indeed I don't! I think she's hideous," Dusty Moth shouted. "Never in all my life have I been so deceived in a person."

"I don't understand how you can say that," Freddie Firefly told him. "But I suppose your idea of beauty may be different from mine—and from many other people's, too. Anyhow, I hope you'll get your appetite back again."

"I don't know about that," said Dusty Moth. "Just now I don't feel as if I ever wanted to taste food again." A shudder passed over him. And he covered his eyes, as if to shut some terrible image from his memory.

"I must leave you now," said Freddie Firefly. "And please don't forget what you promised me. You remember that you said that if I'd show you a picture of Betsy Butterfly you would stop pestering me about her."

"Don't worry about that!" Dusty Moth assured him bitterly. "I shall never mention Betsy Butterfly's name again. I don't want to think of her. But I'm afraid I can never, never get her face out of my mind.... I know—" he added—"I know I shall see it in my dreams. And just think how terrible it will be to wake at midday, out of a sound sleep, with her dreadful face and form haunting me!"

Freddie Firefly couldn't help feeling sorry for the poor chap. But he could think of nothing to do, except to show him Betsy's portrait once more. So he started to raise the picture from the ground, where it still lay face downward. And the moment Dusty Moth saw what he was about he gave a frightful scream—and flew off into the night.

"He's a queer one!" Freddie Firefly mused. "Now, I've always thought Betsy was a fine-looking——" Just then his eyes fell upon the picture for the first time. And Freddie Firefly's mouth fell open in astonishment.

So amazed was he by what he saw that he tumbled right over backwards. And then, scrambling to his feet, he wrapped the rhubarb leaf hastily around the picture and slung it across his back again.

"Jimmy Rabbit has made a terrible mistake!" he groaned, as he started for the duck pond.

Back at the meeting place once more, Freddie Firefly rushed up to Jimmy Rabbit in great excitement.

"Do you know what you did?" he cried. "You brought me the wrong picture. And Dusty Moth has gone shrieking off into the darkness, he was so disappointed. This is not Betsy Butterfly's picture! It's some dreadful-looking caterpillar. And when I glanced at it just now, over in the orchard, it sent a chill all through me."

For the time being Jimmy Rabbit said nothing. At first he had seemed quite upset. But before Freddie had finished speaking he had begun to smile. And then he unwrapped the picture once more and leaned it against a stone, where the moon's rays fell squarely upon it.

"You're mistaken," he informed Freddie then. "This is a picture of Betsy Butterfly. I painted it myself; and I ought to know. As I explained last night, I made it earlier in the summer; and as I said, she has changed somewhat in the meantime. But it's a very good likeness of her as she was once."

"You mean—" gasped Freddie Firefly—"you mean that Betsy Butterfly was once an ugly caterpillar?"

"Why, certainly!" said Jimmy Rabbit. "And so was Dusty Moth, for that matter. Yes! he was a caterpillar himself, once—and a much uglier one than Betsy, if only he knew it.

"In fact," said Jimmy, looking at the picture with his head on one side, "as caterpillars go, Betsy Butterfly was a great beauty, even at so early an age."

XXII

THE SKIPPER

IN Farmer Green's meadow there lived a very nervous person called the Skipper. He was a distant cousin of Betsy Butterfly's. And since the two were almost exactly the same age, they quite naturally spent a good deal of time together.

The Skipper was of a dark, somber brown shade. And it always seemed to the gaily colored Betsy that he tried to make up for his dull appearance by being extremely lively in his movements. He was forever skipping suddenly from one place to another—a trick which had caused people to call him by so odd a name.

Much as she liked this queer cousin, Betsy often found his uncertain habit somewhat annoying. It was not very pleasant, when talking to him, to discover that he had unexpectedly left her when she supposed he was right beside her, or behind her. If she had anything important to tell him she frequently had to hurry after him. And the worst of it was, once she had overtaken him she never knew when he would dart away again.

As the summer lengthened it seemed to Betsy Butterfly that the Skipper grew more flighty than ever. Once she had been able to say a few words to him before he went swooping off. But now—now she could not even tell him that it was a nice day without following her cousin at least half an hour in order to finish her remark.

"You're becoming terribly fidgety," Betsy told him at last. "If you don't look out you'll have nervous prostration—or I shall, if you don't stop jumping about like a jack-in-the-box. I advise you," she said, "to see a doctor before you get any worse."

Of course, it must not be supposed that Betsy Butterfly could say all that to her cousin without going to a good deal of trouble. As a matter of fact, she had to follow him about the fields for two whole days and travel several miles before she succeeded in finishing what she wanted to say to him.

"Why, I feel fine!" the Skipper cried. "I don't need a doctor. I— —"

He started to skip away from the wild morning-glory blossom on which he had perched himself. But Betsy caught him just in time—and held him.

"Now, you listen to me!" she commanded. "You're in a dangerous condition. Some day someone will come to you with an important message. And if you go sailing off the way you do, how's he ever going to tell the whole message until it's too late, perhaps?"

"If it was good news it wouldn't hurt it to keep it a while," the Skipper asserted cheerfully. And he gave a quick spring, with the hope of escaping from Betsy's grasp. But she held him firmly by the coat-tails.

"Suppose I wanted to warn you not to go near the flower garden, because Johnnie Green was waiting there for you with his net, to capture you and put you in his collection? You might be sorry, afterwards, if you didn't sit still and listen to me."

"That's so!" said the Skipper. "I hadn't thought of that. I'd see a doctor at once; but I don't know any."

"Go to Aunt Polly Woodchuck, under the hill," Betsy Butterfly advised him. "She's the best doctor for miles around."

So they went, together, to call on Aunt Polly. The old lady looked at the Skipper and shook her head. "I can't help him," she said.

Betsy asked anxiously, "Is his trouble catching?"

"No, indeed!" said Aunt Polly. "He can't stay in one place long enough to give it to anybody."

Well, after that Betsy saw very little of her cousin the Skipper. But she did not mind that, especially since she soon made the acquaintance of a very agreeable young gentleman, who dressed in the height of fashion. He wore a swallowtail coat every day. And the neighbors all said that his manners were delightful.

He never went skipping off while Betsy Butterfly was talking to him.

THE END

Milton Keynes UK
Ingram Content Group UK Ltd.
UKHW020843260624
444769UK00011B/465

9 781836 572008